So

Amit Chaudhuri is the aut
Sojourn and *Friend of My* 1
essays, three books of poems, a collection of short stories
and a critical study of D. H. Lawrence's poetry. He has re-
ceived the Commonwealth Writers' Prize, the Betty Trask
Prize, the Encore Prize, the *LA Times* Book Prize and the
Sahitya Akademi Award, among other accolades. He is a
Fellow of the Royal Society of Literature. He was Professor
of Contemporary Literature at the University of East An-
glia from 2006 until 2021, and he is Professor of Creative
Writing and Director of the Centre for the Creative and the
Critical, Ashoka University. He edits literaryactivism.com.
He is a vocalist in the North Indian classical tradition and a
composer and performer in a celebrated project that brings
together different musical traditions. *Finding the Raga: An
Improvisation on Indian Music* won the James Tait Black
Prize in 2022.

Further praise for *Sojourn*:

'Chaudhuri is one of the most consistently interesting
writers working today. You get the feeling that with each
book he has to begin again, reconfigure from the ground
up what he wants the novel to be and to do. It's this radical
questioning that makes him such a consistently engaging
writer, and what makes this novel so memorable.' Jon Day,
Financial Times

'Chaudhuri is masterful at showing the effect Berlin has on the narrator . . . Dryness and prosaic charm often punctuate the narrator's inner voice. [W]e are absorbed by the 130 pages of text and its invitation to read between the lines.' Mika Ross-Southall, *The Spectator*

'[A] beautiful meditation on memory set during a temporary stay in Berlin . . . Chaudhuri does not use titles, names or numbers to separate the sections of his narrative. Instead there are generous spaces, including whole blank pages such as these. The effect is similar to that of reading someone's notebook, intimate and fragmentary; but the impressions are not chronologically arranged, as they might be in an actual notebook. They circle round and double back on themselves in an artful way that shows the narrator sinking into a reckoning with Berlin's past, which ends in a series of dizzy spells and an amnesia that includes his own name.' Ruth Scurr, *Times Literary Supplement*

'[U]ltimately a very radical experiment in fiction. It is pared to an essence – but not obviously; the novel rewards re-reading, revealing itself then more clearly to be considerably more in its less-ness . . . certainly, it is a fascinating text.' M. A. Orthofer, *Complete Review*

'*Sojourn* actually makes us rethink what a plot is . . . [it] relies on subtext: the less Chaudhuri says, the more may be intimated . . . A quirk of the German language is that the word for monument, Denkmal, can also be an imperative: "think for a moment". A monument that is also an invitation to reflect, Berlin is a Denkmal to this novel's narrator, just as the novel itself is to its readers.' Tanjil Rashid, *Literary Review*

'As he traverses the city, its fractured lines and history, it's a pleasure to be in his company, like being transported to Berlin . . . full of artful moments, a short, compelling book where every encounter and remark seems charged with significance. The tone of *Sojourn* is ruminative, almost laconic, but the observations throughout the book startle. Chaudhuri is renowned for his style, the clarity of his prose. But he is also a master of figurative language. The book is rich in imagery that estranges then instantly connects . . . [A]n intriguing, thought-provoking read on the pleasures and perils of displacement.' Sarah Gilmartin, *Irish Times*

'It is the lyrical precision of Mr Chaudhuri's writing . . . that truly holds us fast . . . a shimmering present in which we are held spellbound. *Sojourn* maintains a similarly persistent grip . . . that Mr Chaudhuri so effectively creates . . . brilliant.' Anne Mundow, *Wall Street Journal*

'Disorientation arrives in the very first line of *Sojourn* and percolates through this short, memorable book . . . The characters are firmly and evocatively drawn . . . Mr Chaudhuri's writing, limpid and sparse, neatly illustrates [the] struggle to navigate the inner life.' *The Economist*

'Many points in this drifting chronicle are briefly intense, a product of the narrator's close observation and glinting insights. A mere 140 pages, with some holding just one or two paragraphs, the book is only physically slight. It grips the mind, as much with appreciation as with frustration, and teases one into parsing what is real or autofiction, what is changeless or transient. A reader may even enjoy feeling a bit at sea, like the narrator: "I've lost my bearings – not in the city; in its history." A masterful writer in his own subtle, thoughtful, demanding genre.' *Kirkus Reviews* (Starred Review)

'Where most of us can barely trace our own footprints in the mass of moments that are the stuff of experience, numerous and storyless as grains of sand on a beach, Chaudhuri delves in masterfully to lift out arcs, moods, treasures.' James Meek

'I loved *Sojourn*'s evocation of autumnal Berlin, through which a stranger drifts and undergoes a kind of disintegration. This is a mysterious, subtle, haunting novel.' Chris Power

'*Sojourn* is just stunning. I see in its DNA a little bit of Kazuo Ishiguro's mighty *Unconsoled*, but distilled. It's really a piece of music . . . Reading it is like going into a trance.' Neel Mukherjee

'Chaudhuri is a thoughtful writer in a range of genres – he recently won a prize for a book about Indian classical music – and his spare new novel offers a gateway to his distinctive pleasures . . . the novel's shards, glinting with intelligence, are often funny as well as unsettling – the narrator, seemingly, as mysterious to himself as he is to us.' Anthony Cummings, *Daily Mail*

Sojourn

Amit Chaudhuri

faber

First published in 2022
by Faber & Faber Limited
The Bindery
51 Hatton Garden
London ECIN 8DH

This paperback edition first published in 2023

Typeset by Typo•glyphix, Burton-on-Trent, DEI4 3HE
Printed and bound by CPI Group (UK) Ltd, Croydon, CRO 4YY

A CIP record for this book
is available from the British Library

ISBN 978–0–571–36035–2

Printed and bound in the UK on FSC® certified paper in line with our continuing
commitment to ethical business practices, sustainability and the environment.
For further information see faber.co.uk/environmental-policy

2 4 6 8 10 9 7 5 3 1

Sojourn

It was evening, and I didn't know the name of the road I was taken to. It was as if I'd woken from a sleep: maybe because I'd arrived two days ago. I wasn't tired; I was wide awake. But I'd have been lost without my contact. He told me which U-Bahn to take. I got off at Uhlandstrasse and climbed up the stairs. He'd been waiting for me.

At my talk, there was a furtive man. I haven't decided if I mean 'furtive' or 'entertaining'. There's a kind of person who does dramatic things quietly, who pretends they're invisible while blocking the view. It's as if they believe that not being aware of themselves is a guarantee that others can't see them. He was such a person. He stood out because he was Indian, but more because – as if he'd brought something to a wedding he'd now decided to pass off as a gift – he placed a mike on the table. It was as if only he could see the mike; it wasn't the one that had been set up for me to speak into. I let it lie. He went and stood at the back. He had the deprecating manner of a man who knows everything is about himself.

1

At the end of the talk, four or five people came to speak with me, and he elbowed his way through with the air of someone who realises his train has arrived, apologetic, cheerful, pleased with himself.

'Hello!' he said. I heard a Bengali accent. He continued in Bengali. 'Ami aar ki . . . That is, I recorded your talk but I want to ask you some questions. Can I see you tomorrow?' I studied him, dazzled. 'I am from Deutsche Welle!' I didn't know what Deutsche Welle was, but my contact gave it a gravitas-conferring nod. I relented. 'When and where?' I didn't want to sound desperate, but I had few responsibilities. 'I will call you,' he said, without explaining how he had come by my number. He bent forward to give me his card. 'Faqrul – my name,' he said. On the card was 'Faqrul Haq'. 'Deutsche Welle' was in italics.

The next morning I had a dark bread I'd never had before with coffee. I buttered it and ate it untoasted.

The flat was new to me. I'd moved into it the day before yesterday in a hurry. It wasn't the flat I'd arrived into. That was smaller: a kind of studio. The drawing room and bedroom merged with the kitchen. In another mood I would have found it charming. The first evening, though, I was depressed especially by the lack of demarcation between shower and toilet. The bathroom was narrow. On another day, I would have warmed to this. Which space do you own more entirely than the bathroom? But, that evening, I stepped out of the shower and saw the toilet was wet. I called Jonas.

'I hope everything is all right,' he said.

'Yes it is. Yes it is, thank you . . . There's one thing.'

'Please don't hesitate to tell me.'

I tried to remember.

'Isn't it true . . . actually, I have the letter before me. Isn't it true that the Böll Professor gets a two-bedroom flat?'

I could hear Jonas taking this in. I'd only entered the

flat an hour ago. I'd embraced it inwardly. I'd taken to its twentieth-century quality – but then rapidly began to feel doubtful, to reconcile what I'd been asked to expect to where I'd been deposited by Jonas.

'Yes, the Böll Professor gets a two-bedroom flat. That is right.'

'But this is a one-bed, I think . . . or a studio.'
A silence.

'Yes, yes. I see. Yes – I think they thought that since you don't have your *family* with you, you won't need a regular flat.'

'Yes, I understand. The bathroom here is very small, Jonas. It's not what I expected.' I said, knowing he'd now dislike me, 'I can't be here for four months. I think I should get the flat I was promised. I'd rather go back if you can't.'

'No, no, no, no.' I already had a sense that Jonas was courteous and unexcitable. He allowed himself a moment of urgency. 'I will call Max right away.'

Max, who had invited me, was on sabbatical in Arizona.

'Thank you, Jonas.'

I moved the next morning. The Böll Professor's apartment was only two houses away.

4

It was spacious, with wooden floorboards. An expansive drawing room, with a TV near the window. The small bedroom had a bunk bed, presumably for children. I never went there. My room had a king-sized bed: unlikely to be put to full use. To not have a family felt like a windfall. The kitchen was to the left of the hall leading to the front door. There was surplus space here too. I registered this as I buttered my bread the first morning.

The bathroom was almost miraculous. It was wide but long, with a bath and shower. As in a golf course, you felt there was always more to come.

The toilet was a conundrum. I'd never seen anything like it, except in the studio flat. It was mostly a slab, like a dissection table. I decided to acclimatise myself. But I couldn't bear to sit on it for very long. It stained easily because of the shape, and I started cleaning it as soon as I began using it. I wondered if it was part of an industrial heritage.

Using that toilet, my first thought was, 'Oe must have sat here.' He couldn't have escaped it. And I felt a kind of

5

empathy and embarrassment thinking of Kenzaburo Oe in this bathroom, seated where I was, of him then going out to the drawing room. Oe had won the Nobel Prize, but this is what it comes back to: our relief at amenities.

Jonas had told me that Oe had occupied the flat in the late nineties before it began to be assigned to Böll Visiting Professors. He'd spent six months in Berlin at the invitation of the German Academic Exchange Service. I had read one Oe novel – by chance, recently. It was about a man and his brain-damaged son, a seemingly insentient being who's also a living conscience. It had been mentioned by a relative who himself was terribly bereaved: his son had killed himself. Oe's novel was, I heard, drawn from life. All this – the relative; Oe's suffering; my bum touching the seat that Oe's had rested on – was on my mind in my first days in the flat.

The cell phone rang late in the morning. 'Hello!' said the voice. 'Hello!' I said. It was like an old-fashioned trunk call. 'Hello kemon achho!' I was rapt for a second. 'Faqrul, aar ki.' I'd forgotten our conversation. I'd forgotten about the talk last night. 'We said we'd meet today?' The reluctance in my silence may have been audible. He was a man who expected reluctance. He had a bridegroom's thick skin. 'I was thinking of getting some work done. What is it that you'd like to do?' 'Oh, nothing at all! An interview for Deutsche Welle, what else. We will have lunch. I will introduce you to a fantastic place. I will show you two or three fantastic places, but we can start today.' My suspicion increased. 'Fantastic place meaning . . . ?' He brushed me off. 'You wait and see! I'll tell you how to get there.'

He said I should walk to Oskar-Helene-Heim and take the U-Bahn to Görlitzer Bahnhof. I made him spell the name, because the way he said it – 'gollitza banhoff' – had me guessing. He was clearly a local. A Bengali local.

———

Görlitzer Bahnhof is old. I don't mean that it's getting on in years. I mean it's familiar. Just as when you say 'He's an old friend of mine' you're talking not about the friend's age but that he's been your friend for a long time, Görlitzer Bahnhof felt known to me. It was my second time in Berlin; I had little memory of the first visit. I should add that the U-Bahn is misleadingly named. It's hardly an underground line. Much of it floats over the city. Görlitzer Bahnhof is itself elevated.

As I came down the stairs I saw a man in an ash-coloured plastic jacket smoking furiously. I'd forgotten what Faqrul looked like, but he smiled at me and I smiled back distantly. He had the huddled look of a man who likes snatching time to himself. 'Be careful, they're all pickpockets,' he said. Africans had been waiting for me to descend. 'Esho,' he said, navigating. He was shorter and older than me. He wore thick glasses and had a moustache. He was strong.

We crossed the road. I wondered what we'd eat. He had a pre-emptive air: of someone who not only knew me for years, but could predict my questions. After seven or eight minutes, we came to an Indian restaurant. We went up the steps and entered a large yellow space. It had a luncher: an old man. Faqrul introduced me to a plump young man. 'Here's the person I was telling you about.' The plump man ushered me in the way a prince of a small state might show the dignitary of a major nation his modest palace.

Pakoras and mango lassi arrived. 'Should we do the interview now or later?' asked Faqrul. 'Thhaak, let's eat first!' 'Yes, we can do it later. If we don't fall asleep after the meal.' Faqrul's compact being shook with laughter. The plump proprietor asked pointedly: 'Tandoori prawn khaiben?' I don't like prawns in Indian restaurants in Europe because they're frozen, but they were his most prized gift and I nodded.

I admit I was a bit disappointed. I didn't expect to be having Indian food in Berlin on my fourth day. I asked:

'Have you heard of Himalaya Imbiss?'

'Himalaya Imbiss?'

Faqrul had a deep voice – suited for radio.

'A friend mentioned it.'

'A friend? Achha?'

I was thinking of Adhir Roy; a sociologist and misfit. He'd been here in 1987. When I told him I was off to Berlin, he'd gone into a reverie. 'You must go to Himalaya Imbiss,' he said. 'It's a small place. *Very* nice. You can get curry there. I'd sit there for hours.'

'His name's Adhir Roy.'

'Adhir Roy . . .'

Faqrul frowned with the authority of one who's on first-name terms with everyone worth knowing in Calcutta, though he hadn't visited it in forty years.

'No, don't know him,' he said.

Then he addressed the proprietor, who happened to be passing:

'Afzal! Do you know Himalaya Imbiss?'

'Himalaya . . .' said Afzal, with a practised blankness. In my head, Himalaya Imbiss had become the only place in West Berlin in 1987 that served Indian food. It came back to me that Adhir Roy hadn't lived in Berlin in 1987, but 1989. But any history before November 1989 was so continuous that Adhir could be embedded in it in any point. That was eternity – with its Himalaya Imbisses, never to pass. Adhir was a film fanatic – he'd come to Berlin to pursue Alexander Kluge, both the man and his work. He told me that he'd been to dinner with a Left–Green group the day before people were given licence to clamber over the wall. 'None of us knew,' he said, 'that it would end. When it did end the next day, it felt inevitable.'

There was a wave of food: chicken bhuna, daal, pilau rice, tandoori prawns. Soon I'd find out that lunch was gratis. Faqrul – I didn't know it then – was a well-known exile. He was a poet, booted out of Bangladesh in 1975 for insulting the Prophet Muhammad in a poem. Buoyed by blasphemy, he'd gone to a careless extreme. His imagery was scatological. He found refuge in Calcutta. There, he became a literary scene regular. Then the West Bengal government, belatedly nervous, or realising the poem had denigrated every known deity, reconsidered his domicile. Around this time, Günter Grass was in Calcutta, discovering, Columbus-like, its garbage heaps and poor. He hung out with writers, heard of Faqrul's tenuous situation. He must have liked him, because he began making arrangements for Faqrul to get asylum. Faqrul emigrated to Germany in 1977. I wasn't non-plussed by the waiving of the bill, as I knew of the gener-osity of the Bangladeshis. I didn't know then that Faqrul

– despite his beliefs or lack of them, despite the infamy that had descended on him in 1975 or because of it – was held in awe by proprietors of Indian restaurants across Berlin, all God-fearing Bangladeshis. They periodically served lavish meals free to Faqrul and his distinguished visitors, among whom I suppose I was included.

After lunch, Faqrul held a large microphone while I spoke about modernity's advent in the world – the subject of my last book and the next one.

Outside, the sky was pale. 'This is Kreuzberg!' Faqrul announced. 'That way no man's land,' he said, wheeling around for a second. We resumed walking, staying parallel to the overhead bridge of Görlitzer Bahnhof. I stopped to study a Mercedes-Benz; it was a model I'd seen and even got into as a child, a 250. It looked unaffected by the seasons. Behind it was a small car: the excitement of confronting something you don't know is very like the excitement of recognising something you were familiar with long ago. 'What is this?' I asked. It was new to me, and incredibly old. Faqrul tried reading its name, but I think he was bluffing when he said: 'It's an East German model.' There was a hint of pleasure in his words. It could have been a Soviet make. Self-sufficient, redundant.

'Come,' said Faqrul, beckoning. He'd stopped before a board. It had flyers pinned to it. 'See,' he said. I flinched.

It was a photograph of a nude woman. I flinched not because it was obscene. But what did he have in mind? Was this an avuncular initiation? The photo was black and white. The woman's outlines – breasts, shoulders – were rounded, soft. It was from 1923. I could guess at enough of the text to understand it announced an exhibition of erotic pictures from the time. 'See?' said Faqrul; I paused at the eyebrows, pale nipples, and navel. 1923 meant nothing; the woman was in a 'now' and all else was irrelevant. 'And this one,' he said, pointing to another poster. 'Off-theatre. Something out of the way.' I didn't know what the poster said. I imagined what 'off-theatre' implied. 'This board,' he said, gesturing with a hand, 'is for off-theatre.'

There was a U-Bahn to the university – the stop was named after it – but it was more straightforward to walk. Once out of the U-Bahn you had to get your bearings. With the road, you kept going till you came to a fork – then you went right.

The university had come up in the fifties, but large bits were recent. The long corridor felt like a provincial airport: constant arrivals, departures, long delays. Students could take seven years to do their MAs – a reaction against fascism's timekeeping. I dawdled in twice a week. I usually stopped by Jonas's office. He accompanied me to mine. Sometimes, because I was Böll Professor, he introduced me to a luminary in the department. History and Culture had eminent faculty. It was on the first floor.

My office had a telephone and computer and table, and a view of other windows. I used it a few times to meet students, but mostly it was a green room to my weekly lecture. Or it was a waiting room in which I filled in forms which I then handed to my neighbour, the department's head of admin.

———

In my first weeks, I had lunches in the cafeteria. It was a huge space – even when it was crowded, it was never full. At the end of the first week, I was scanning tables, wondering where to sit, and a pretty girl smiled at me before she sat down with her boyfriend, who was eating, oblivious. It occurred to me that she'd smiled as I'd entered the doorway. I speculated if she was a student in History and Culture and had recognised me. Unlikely. It could be she was trying to make me feel at home.

I was a semi-student in the cafeteria. But, in my second week, I gave my inaugural talk, with faculty, students and – I expect – people who were neither in the audience. Jonas introduced me: as they'd invited me to be Böll Professor, they had to pretend I was a scholar of significance. I rambled on why India was a 'modern' idea, not a colonial or postcolonial one, while a woman in the front row nodded, eyes sparkling.

'I teach postcolonial studies myself,' she said – part confession, part dry observation – when she came up later. I realised I may have misread her nods.

'I love your work. I taught your new book to my class last year.'

My heart beat faster, as it does when I hear such words. It's like being caught out. You write for others, in theory; confirmation of the fact is disconcerting.

'That's kind of you,' I said. I left a question unasked, but she picked it up.

'I'm Geeta Roy,' she said.

'Geeta Roy . . .' I weighed the foreignness of the words.

16

'Yes, my father's from Calcutta. My mother is German.'

That explained the eyes' refracted quality, why they'd shone from a distance.

'Look, there are others waiting to talk. Maybe we could meet later. My husband and I would love to take you to dinner.'

'That would be wonderful.'

'You live in Dahlem, don't you? We need to take you out of Dahlem.'

I was discovering that the area I lived in was known for its dullness. You don't make such distinctions on arrival; they're reported to you. They sink in; you think, 'They're right.' The dullness was historical. Dahlem had been created by the Americans to exemplify suburban tranquillity. But its edge intersected, Faqrul had pointed out to me, with Grunewald. I'd glimpsed the forest on my way in from the airport. 'From there they sent Jews to the camps,' he said, lighting a cigarette. Grunewald's frozen beauty felt like it would melt and rush towards Dahlem.

I needed a new jacket. With oncoming autumn, the days were clear but no longer warm. The jacket I had was six years old, and I decided my Böll professorship's stipend was an excuse to get a new one.

'Bhabchhi ekta jacket kinbo,' I said to Faqrul. He'd begun to call me every day.

'You come to Wittenbergplatz,' he instructed me.

'Where are you?' I said on the phone.

He was in front of a self-service tea shop.

'Will you have tea first, or later?'

'Later is fine. I'm a bit hungry now, but tea can wait.'

He gestured to me to pause and went in. He came out after five minutes with a doughnut.

'Hold this,' he said, handing me the paper bag.

Then he jumped back in at the entrance and said something to a man sitting on a stool, looking out on the street. 'Bitte, bitte,' he said, cigarette pointed. What I could overhear – 'schön', 'ach so', 'danke', other words I couldn't follow – sounded exactly like Bengali.

'I forgot the lighter at home,' he chuckled, exhaling smoke.

'Where's the place?' I asked him. I'd eaten half the doughnut.

'Oh, nearby. Two minutes.'

Two evenings later he took me where, if you walked further up, the Brandenburg Gate and the Reichstag were visible. The road was bright with lights. Everywhere were flat stones, like rockery on an abandoned shore.

'These,' said Faqrul, 'are to remember the Jews.' He spoke in an offhand way, puffed up with a sense of accomplishment. In and out we went through the shadows of what was part graveyard, part playground.

'I was beaten up here,' he said – again, exuding satisfaction.

'*What?* When?'

We paused at a stone.

'1992. I was wandering around when a bunch of thugs came by. Oi – neo-Nazi . . .'

'Where did neo-Nazis come from?' I laughed in disbelief. '*Here* of all places?'

'Oi je,' he said, turning his head towards Brandenburg Gate. 'They lived not far away. The East was *full* of neo-Nazis.'

'What happened?'

A couple walked past, politely looking away.

'Oi aar ki. One of them said, "Was machst du hier?"' He let a heavy Bengali cadence embrace the words. 'Maaney, what are you doing here?'

He bowed and lit a cigarette.

'I said, "Was geht's dich an?"' He mangled the syllables with relish. 'Maaney, tor ki hoyechhe re? What's it to *you*?'

'*What?* Faqrul, don't you know you should *ignore* people like that? You don't make eye contact with Nazis, let alone respond to them!'

He ducked, incorrigible, in repentance. His body rocked. Because he was a smoker, the laughter was like a kettle's hiss. It filled the dark space.

'They beat me up,' he said. 'I remember nothing. When I woke up I was in a police station.'

'At least they didn't kill you.'

'I lost all my teeth.'

'Your teeth? What are those, then?' I said, peering at his mouth.

We began to proceed from that faux-cemetery towards Tiergarten.

'Dentures.'

'Those teeth aren't yours?'

'No.' Once more, a surge of self-satisfaction. 'I lost mine in 1992.'

That jacket! A pale green that shone. When I say 'shone'
I mean a subdued resplendence. Not quite tweedy, but
textured, like a surface.

'What do you think?' I'd said, admiring my likeness.

'Take it,' Faqrul said. 'It suits you.'

So I bought it. I didn't know then it would be indestruct-
ible. Styles might change, but German things don't
spoil. We went down to the escalator.

At Peek and Cloppenburg that day I was billed on the third floor and went down to the second to pay. There was a small queue before me; women waiting to finish their purchases. The coat had descended a floor. The parcel was handed over by the cashier.

'This is like India,' I said to Faqrul as we departed via the main foyer. Parcels would be left by an emissary, or lowered down by a string in plain view.

I came to Wittenbergplatz every other day and ate with Faqrul – at the buffet in the Europa Center's basement. Faqrul sought out basements, or we had tea on a stool on the first floor of a department store from where you could survey the street.

The food was cheap because the city was bankrupt. The Americans had waited for an invasion: it never happened. As a result, there had been no accumulation of capital.

You could buy bits of the wall. Faqrul knew those who manned the kiosks between Uhlandstrasse and

Wittenbergplatz. The kiosks were like bunkers. Self-sufficient. They displayed key rings, bottles, magazines, cigarettes. Faqrul brandished me to the vendors, as he had in Kreuzberg. The men received me with shy approval; the way bridegrooms are. They were Iranians, Afghans, Bangladeshis. Faqrul always bought, or was gifted, a bottle of mineral water. He would have been well known to them as the poet who'd been thrown out of his homeland. It didn't look like they minded. In my first month, I pored the fragments of the wall in the kiosks for genuineness. It was fifteen years since the wall had fallen but it seemed there was an inexhaustible supply.

Sometimes we stood near Wittenbergplatz station and had bratwurst or würstchen. It was Faqrul who'd broached the matter. 'Würstchen,' he'd said. 'Chalo, we'll meet at Wittenbergplatz at 12.30.' We stood in the sun, our mouths full. I said, 'This is pork, right?' – concerned whether he knew. 'Oh yes!' He combined a brief laugh with the serious business of chewing. Eating bratwurst was an extension of insulting Allah. He found it delicious on many levels – like a Christian placing the host on his tongue. Blasphemy is a religious experience.

I went to Peek and Cloppenburg again with Faqrul to buy a sweater. 'Chalo, kadiway jabe,' he muttered. 'What?' 'Maaney, ka – di – way,' he said, tilting his head. KaDeWe was next door, looming like a cinema. Faqrul took me straight to the food hall at the top. Sausages hung here, and people served themselves helpings of white or green asparagus. We didn't eat – we moved and stared.

When I explored the Jewish Museum with Jonas two months later (what a trip that was – I lost my way and was late and had to run; the museum was closing and Jonas was angry) – it was there I confronted the journeys the Jews had made. Families that had been wiped out had left behind a handkerchief, or a doll, or a photo album. The Jews came after the grandeur of the nineteenth century – the last age of the monarchs. They were nothing if not ordinary; recognisable. I knew them.

The owners of KaDeWe would have been deported to one camp or another; the store was gutted in the war. All this made sense to me that day in the museum. After all, weren't department stores the century's cathedrals? And is it any surprise that they should be destroyed? I had a sense of confirmation.

Where had Faqrul taken me? If KaDeWe had gone, what did we see?

A woman came to clean the flat on Fridays. She was in her mid-sixties. I felt guilty she had to do the work, but she was robust. She wore a white dress, and she beamed. From her warmth, and the fact that she didn't know a word of English, I deduced she was from the East. I managed to extract from her – how, I don't know, because I don't know German – that she lived beyond Kreuzberg. We had conversations underlined by nods and smiles about the weather, the flat, the bathroom, each other's health.

'What are you doing this weekend?' She elaborated on something animatedly. I smiled in agreement. Before she resumed cleaning, we both shook our heads from side to side at the state of the world.

On my last trip to Berlin – my first visit – I was taken to Kreuzberg to eat a Turkish meal by an academic and was later shown the 'prefabricated flats' workers in the GDR had lived in. Most still lived there. The balconies were bright blue. He said that Easterners knew no English.

On Gerta's arrival (that was her name), I'd think of blue buildings.

Right next to Oskar-Helene-Heim station is an imbiss. I never saw it closed. I stopped to check its name. It dispensed currywurst, fries. I didn't go in.

As Faqrul met me at pre-appointed spots, he never came by my apartment. But he was unsurprised when I mentioned the bedrooms, the bathroom's spaciousness, and empathised when I confessed to my self-consciousness sitting on the toilet Oe had sat upon. I think he'd been to the flat in the tenure of another Böll Professor.

He invited me to his flat for dinner. It was a two-bedroom on Eisenacher Strasse. The walls were lined with books, among which was a volume of nude photos of Madonna. He encouraged me to look. I turned its pages as he went in to get food. I found a photograph on the shelf, of a long-haired man, a child in his arms. Faqrul returned with a bowl of rice. 'That's me,' he explained, with the kind of pride a father takes in a son. 'With my nephew.' 'You?' I juxtaposed person with image. The man was smiling, and I realised I was looking at Faqrul's real teeth. 'Here you're *really* looking like a poet,' I said. His shoulders shook as he laughed, incredulous.

The doorbell buzzed when we began to eat.

'That must be Christiana,' muttered Faqrul. He prodded the daal. 'Take, take,' he instructed.

He went to open the door. A woman entered after two minutes.

'Amar bandhobi.' I don't know what Christiana made of this. She was warm-looking – in her fifties, with frizzy hair. But Faqrul had already told me he had a bandhobi – an Englishwoman called Miriam.

'Hi Christiana,' I said. She seemed amused.

'I've heard about you from Faqrul.'

'Christiana is in the World Bank,' said Faqrul in his radio voice. 'She gets held up at meetings.'

'Faq-rul! Such a lavish spread! When did you find the time?' She was from the East Coast.

Faqrul shrugged casually, like a patriarch.

When I saw him again, I said:

'Didn't you say your bandhobi is called Miriam?'

'Miri-yam,' he said with affection.

'Who's Christiana?'

He chuckled, like an adult being challenged by a child over a magic trick.

'Christiana is a *very* old friend.'

'Bandhobi in what sense?'

'Well, she's a woman, isn't she? A woman . . . friend.' He said, 'Sometimes we – aar ki . . .'

Noticing my disbelief, he added: 'You can have her if you want.'

Faqrul – in the excitement of being in your company – was a man who liked to share. He gave you food; he stood next to you in solidarity when you tried on jackets; he would have shared cigarettes and his flat if I'd been a smoker or needed a room; he might offer his woman. He didn't create a boundary round himself, saying, 'This is mine; not yours.' As long as he was with you, he was in a state of transport. Walking towards Zoologischer Garten, he waved to the doors on the left and said, 'You want to go in?' I hadn't noticed the sex shop, so unprepossessing was the entrance. I wondered, 'Who is this man? Pandarus?' Then I realised – he's giving me the benefit of the doubt, in case I'm the kind of yokel he was when he arrived. The first time, I demurred; but the second time I did go in, as if I were dropping into a supermarket to get some cheese.

His bandhobi's name wasn't Christiana.

A week after the dinner, Faqrul said: 'Come to Potsdamer Platz. The World Bank's throwing a party. Christiana has invited me.'

'But I'm not invited!'

'Oh, leave all that, she was asking after you! And there are free snacks.'

That decided it. I went, as told, to the tenth floor of a glass-fronted building. Faqrul and I surveyed stretches of Potsdamer Platz, eating canapés. A crowd circulated behind us.

'Over there,' he said, pointing, as if at an imaginary cross on a map, munching on remnants, 'is Hitler's bunker.' He was waiting for something to happen. 'From there,' he said, scratching the air's surface, 'they'd go to that hotel opposite to eat. Otherwise, the food would travel across the stretch, which was being shelled.' He sounded like he was recounting arrangements made for a holiday.

Christiana and I found each other. Later: 'Sorry, but have I got your name right?' I thought I'd heard it being said differently in the party.

'It's Kirsten,' she said.

'I'm so *sorry*! Then why—'

'I've *told* Faqrul it's Kirsten,' she giggled. We could see him, hovering surreptitiously by the canapés. 'He forgets.'

He vanished for a fortnight after helping me buy new shoes.

It was mid-October. I wore my new jacket everywhere. I phoned him.

'I heard winters in Germany are cold.'

'Quite cold.' Matter-of-fact; no argument here.

'Do you know where I should get heavy shoes? The shoes I'm wearing won't be good in the snow.'

'Kalke Wittenbergplatze eshe jao.'

So, next day, I went. He was in front of the shop he'd directed me to. It's not as if I was late. Faqrul always arrives early. He stands at entrances, smoking.

We went to the basement and I tried on shoes lined with fur. The tips were rounded. They emanated a native sorrow. If feet have souls, mine were unprepared for the warmth in which they found themselves. I plodded around.

'You think they'll do?'

'They're good,' he said, narrowing his eyes like he was assessing weaponry.

Then he disappeared for two weeks. Unavailable on the phone.

But, prior to the shoes-purchase, we met up at Friedrichstrasse.

'Chalo, chalo,' he said. 'Just change at Hallesches Tor for Oranien-boorger Tor.'

He was already there. A sunlit Sunday. We walked up in the heat and waited for a tram. We hopped on and he told me not to pay. He had no ticket either. Sometimes he'd carry a sheaf of them, like a proselytiser. We hopped off after five minutes.

We crossed the road. I felt a deep sense of home-coming. I didn't know where we were. I wanted to go deeper. We stood in front of a building, fugitive; Faqrul blurted out, 'Eta aar ki, *Neu* synagogue.' He said 'Neu' like the Bangla nine. 'The men, aar ki, came and burnt it.' He sounded disbelieving despite himself. I was gripped by foreboding. 'What am I doing here?' Yet there was nowhere I'd rather have been. 'Kristallnacht . . . They smashed the glass on 9th November.' We were standing under branches; the trees are expansive here. I grew so absorbed for an instant I didn't know who I was. '9th November,' he murmured. Then, bored, he turned left, facing the way we'd come.

We had würstchen and poached on the environs. From Oranienburger Strasse we progressed to Hackescher Markt. Faqrul maintained his furtiveness – the air of being prepared for everything. In one of the by-lanes – (was it that day or another one?) I think it was in Prenzlauer Berg – he pointed to the indentation in the stone on a balcony. 'Bullet,' he said. The English word was agitating; I peered, blind. Was he making it up? I had a feeling that, just as his idea of privacy was subjective, so was his truth. To access history in this way, you had to access *him*.

I'd come here before. When, I'm not sure. I knew the neighbourhoods: gates, doorways. I let Faqrul do the talking.

They go on about the rebarbative sound German makes, but individual words and names have greater beauty – more history – than English can carry. I entered Hackescher Markt in my mind's eye five or ten minutes before reaching there. 'Friedrichstrasse'

38

had come up in a dream recently, as a port of arrival. Kristallnacht was transparent, broken. I woke up to words and didn't bother with the language.

'See those.'

On the fringes of Hackescher Markt we slipped through a passage. I thought it was a shortcut. He was pointing to the stones. It was a bit of metal that concerned him, an ore where the stone had scraped off.

'Their names,' he said.

There was more than one. They were scattered but immovable. Each had a name and nickname and dates: everything in a life. You had to squint to see.

'What . . .'

'These people,' said Faqrul, glancing at the apartments. What did he mean by this drama: 'these people'? Those who lived here now couldn't possibly be those who'd lived here then; they couldn't even be descendants. Yet they were hidden, like the original owners. There was no sign of them. They seemed to be waiting. We were looking for them, as others had before us.

In the university cafeteria, I met a Canadian called Simons. 'May I?' he said, hesitating, and I of course said yes, and he lowered his tray before me. We began to converse over loaded plates.

He was a political scientist from Toronto. He seemed reminiscent of Professor Alembick in *King Ottokar's Sceptre* – not as sprightly, but bearded, short-sighted. He introduced himself as Peter.

I asked him if he knew of Partha Chatterjee – he reminded me of Partha Chatterjee too.

'Oh yes,' he nodded, as if I'd mentioned a health-giving herb.

It turned out he was in the same block of flats I was in: not the same building; the same block.

'What's it like?'

'It's nice,' he said, forking up macaroni. 'Small, you know, but perfectly OK.'

'A one-bed?'

'No,' he said, mournful and content. 'It's a studio.'

'Ah, I've seen those.'

I didn't bring up the shower that made the bathroom wet. I would have liked his opinion on the toilet, whose plateau continued to vex me in the morning.

He was here to do proper research for a year: unlike me, an ornament to an internationalisation initiative. Over another lunch a week later, we discussed politics while navigating gunk with forks. Though he was at least fifteen years older, neither of us had expected this epoch we lived in.

'The Soviet Union,' I said, 'was a reminder that another order was possible. You may not have *liked* that order, but the fact it existed meant something.'

'Yes,' he murmured.

We went deep into homesickness, a kind of lostness that had come over some people in the last decade.

'And the Soviet Union allowed *our* order to have pockets in it that mirrored it,' I said, biting a soggy chip, 'pockets that needn't have any political affinities with it, but which existed simply because the idea of another order was still valid.'

His mouth was open. The cafeteria was loud.

I saw him a week later, in an Italian restaurant I'd frequent in Dahlem. I used to eat there alone – mostly a bowl of frutti di mare. I'd tell them to add chilli oil, and they'd note this with contempt, as the kind of request to be expected from an Indian.

I hated the three euros they put on the bill because of their insistence on giving me bottled water when I needed water. I said 'tap water' in English a few times, but didn't want to offend them. When Geeta Roy came again to one of my seminars, I said immediately: 'Don't Germans drink tap water? Must I pay for mineral water when I go to a restaurant?' 'Ah!' she smiled – having grown up in Calcutta, she had an eye for German customs – 'say "Leitungswasser". That should do the trick.' 'Sorry, what?' 'Leitungswasser,' she said, patient, apologetic. I repeated the word, till it became less unwieldy, though not less odd, then took it like a mantra that night to the restaurant. 'Leitungswasser,' I said. They declined to understand. The Italians were ingratiating to Germans but obtuse with me. In a manner that had no connection to what I'd said, he returned with a glass of water and put it down reluctantly.

I was going to dive into the frutti di mare when I sensed a figure by my side. It was Professor Simons, on his way out.

'How are you?' He was delighted to have found me.

'I'm well, thank you . . . Nice restaurant,' I said. 'I come here sometimes.'

'It is,' he nodded.

It occurred to me that we were both Dahlemites – though there's probably no such word.

'Would you . . .' He dithered. He took in a short, gracious breath, started again. 'Would you care to have coffee next week?'

'Yes! That would be nice.'

'We could go,' he said, combining the political scientist's instinct with a boy's simplicity, 'to Tempelhof Airport.'

'The disused one?'

'Yes.'

'That's a good idea!'

He waved cautiously. I went back to the seafood. I couldn't fathom why so many airports in Berlin abdicated their responsibility to perform a function!

To be a Dahlemite is to be seized by a need for adventure. This took us to Tempelhof. You're allowed, in Berlin, to gaze at buildings. It's not an activity that's officially recognised, yet it requires no apology.

'Strange . . .' I said.

It was lit up from within; it gleamed.

'Do you remember,' I said, turning to him, 'how exciting air travel used to be?'

'Yes!'

'It's just coming back to me.'

'Yes,' he said, looking at the airport. Here there's little to separate endings from beginnings, the contemplation of what's lapsed from a strong sense of imminence. 'The packing-up – the pilots and air hostesses – the people coming to see you off – so glamorous!'

We had coffee on the pavement outside a place too small to be called a café. In fact, *he* had coffee. I had Fanta. It was like summer.

I was sitting alone in the evening, watching TV. There was nothing to watch – the only channels I followed were CNN and BBC. I pored over the news – the burning and rioting outside Paris, the swarms of youth and black armies of policemen. From the BBC I turned sometimes to *Heimat*, which had been going on forever: its ambition appeared to be to rival, in longevity, the history it was recording. It was peacetime in *Heimat*. I stayed with the inexplicable images, of people drinking beer in the sun, of movement inside rooms, interminable conversations. I didn't know which year it was – there was no ostensible period detail; everything was humdrum, 'normal' – 1970; 1980?

Heimat absorbed me three days into my visit. I still hadn't seen Berlin – nothing but the station at Uhlandstrasse and the bookstore. And yet I felt drawn – I watched without comprehension, recognising something in bits of each episode.

Then, two days later, when I was having dinner on the sofa, I caught an oddity switching channels. Shahrukh Khan. It was 9.30: prime time. He was talking in German. There were two of him: one sat at a distance from the other.

At the end of my third weekly seminar, I was walking towards Dahlem-Dorf station, a fairy-tale building. A woman who'd been sitting in on my classes was with me. She was tall and quiet, but not shy. She was a PhD student in Philology. I asked her if it was a popular subject.

'Oh yes!' she said. 'It's important in Germany.'
The gable at the road's end grew larger.
'I'm so sorry, I've forgotten your name.'
'It's Petra.'
'Petra!' I thought of my student days; film societies. *The Bitter Tears of Petra von Kant*!'
'Sorry?'
'The Fassbinder film? You know the one I mean?'
She smiled at the footpath.

'You've heard of Fassbinder?'

'I think so . . .' she murmured.

We fell silent. I said:

'Do you know – I came upon a Shahrukh Khan movie the other night. I think it was *Veer-Zaara*. On TV! Have you heard of him?'

This enlivened and provoked her.

'Shahrukh Khan's very popular here!'

'Really?'

I must have sounded scandalised. She glanced at me with a vigorous nod.

'Yes. We have a Bollywood night every Friday. Would you like to come?'

'Bollywood night? What's that?'

'We listen to music. We dance a little.'

'Oh, I see . . . I don't know . . .'

She laughed and dived into the U-Bahn. Dogged, I took the road going left.

Then began my Faqrul-less days. He wouldn't pick up calls. I didn't resent his silence. He'd always felt to me the type who'd retreat, unannounced. He was also the sort who'd reappear, obeying some directive.

One afternoon, Geeta Roy took me out for lunch and we entered a verdant neighbourhood and, driving past, she said, 'That's Günter Grass's house.' I may be wrong, but I think it was pale green. Or could it be my memory's tricking me, and his name, who knows, may have something to do with it. But it wasn't a grassy green: there was just a hint of colour. 'He doesn't live there now,' she said. 'But he did, for years.'

I knew the house already, because these 'years' was the time that Faqrul had lived with Grass. They'd fallen out because he found he was washing too many dishes and writing too little poetry. Grass, too, had had enough to do by then with Faqrul: the tall tales; the exaggerated enthusiasms.

Here, as we drove past, Faqrul's absence in the last

fortnight intersected with Grass's departure from his house for a new one, and with Faqrul's double loss of habitation – not to mention his leech-like optimism and tenacity.

Alone, I went to Peek and Cloppenburg for a winter jacket. The stores are lit like cathedrals in November, but the crowds vying to get in are like droves around temples: intemperate, slightly frivolous. On the third floor, I found an oasis among rows of winterwear. Standing in front of a slanted mirror, I tried a jacket that zipped right to my chin, though I wasn't sure if it fit. 'This one's fetching,' said a man going past; from his appearance I realised after a second he was Pakistani. I like running into Pakistanis abroad: it's like encountering a race of human being that has so much more finesse than you could have. 'You don't think I need a size smaller?' I was seeking him out though I was still drawn to the mirror. 'No,' he said, further off now. 'It's just right.'

Petra dropped out of my class. Its composition was changing. People alighted, got off. As on a raft, a ragged bunch remained: an Israeli student with an American accent; a stocky woman, the kind that's always shopping for groceries; two Indian students from Delhi; a German TA who circulated photocopies; some others, whom I wasn't certain of having seen before.

No one volunteered an opinion. The waters surrounding the raft lay becalmed. At a departmental do, Geeta Roy told me German students liked to defer to authority. Her implication was that the deference was historical, but it made life on the raft difficult, because I held forth but wasn't authoritative. I wanted to hear their shaky English. German students could subsist like this for years, I heard.

'You poor man!' said Geeta.
She commiserated with me for having to steer the seminar and for living in Dahlem.

I got the department to procure a DVD player for me. 'I need to watch TV,' I said. 'I'm tiring of news on the BBC.'

———

In the apartment, I led a life of outward boredom, but never completely disconnected from the edges: Grunewald. Part of me was susceptible to what was outside the pavement and beyond the motorway.

Geeta and her husband drove up to my place with gifts: two DVDs. One was *Rope* (I'd said I didn't want to watch new films). The other was a wildlife documentary which she insisted would soothe and educate me.

We got into the car. We drove, where else, East.

'We'll show you a bit of the city,' Geeta said from the back, ebullient.

'Tell me' – I was peering into the rear-view mirror – 'what exactly is *Heimat*?'

'It's a kind of soap opera,' said Geeta. 'The Germans love it!' I heard tolerant dismissal in her voice. Michael, a hefty newspaperman, dapper but no-nonsense, smiled at the mention of 'the Germans'.

'I've watched a few episodes,' I said. 'I dip in and out.'

'Do you know German?'

'Not a word.'

I added:

'It doesn't matter. I only watch bits of episodes, as you might look out of a window.'

'Haven't seen it in years,' muttered Michael, slowing down at a traffic light.

'It doesn't *seem* like a soap opera,' I said, turning to Geeta despite the seat belt's restraint. 'Not like a British or American one. You know, *EastEnders*. *The Bold and the Beautiful*.'

No, it was more a national autobiography, if there's such a thing. Only the Germans would have used such a device – that is, have their nation recount its memories of growing older in a soap opera. Slip in what's intimate in a way that's unworthy of attention.

The Brandenburg Gate came up. Lit, resplendent, a sovereign without purpose.

'But what did they *do* in the East?' I asked.

'Do?'

'I mean every day.'

Michael told me about the queues; the dreadful food in restaurants. The speaking in whispers, behind closed doors.

'But they must have been happy *some* time?' Each fact brought up an image: of streets; women walking with determination. But something was missing. No human can be unhappy without interruption.

'I think they used to tell each other stories,' said Geeta from the back. 'That's what I've heard. That they'd get together in a room, and recount family stories to keep their spirits up. They'd also sing to each other in the rooms, and dance.'

Maybe I'd misused the word 'happy'. I hadn't meant high spirits or laughter. I had something basic in mind: the release from the awareness of who or where you are, which comes to us a few times a day. To even be in a state when the thought – 'I'm in East Berlin in 1983' – hasn't formed; when consciousness is undecided. It was in imagining that blankness that I felt I could enter the GDR; in reliving the distraction from what's at hand, I became one with it for a few moments.

We ate pasta. Once the sightless avenues around Brandenburg Gate shrink, you're suddenly in a small town. This is the East.

I recounted the anguish of my arrival to Michael.

'The bathroom got wet when you had a shower! Why didn't they put me up in the flat I was *supposed* to get if it was available?'

Michael was eating schnitzel.

'They think you live in a hut,' he said, sectioning, 'where you come from.' Done, like a surgeon washing his hands, he became aware of me. 'They think: *This* is good enough for *him*!' He shrugged, resumed poking at the pieces.

Back in the car, Geeta said of me to Michael:

'He has a question.'

I was confused for a moment. Then I took her cue.

'Ah yes. The toilets with the flat base. I find them intriguing. Are they peculiar to Berlin or the whole of Germany?'

Michael stared at the windshield. He could grow absorbed quickly.

'All of Germany, I think.'

'But that shape? I haven't seen it elsewhere.'

'Don't you know,' sang Geeta, triumphant, 'that Germans like to inspect their poo?'

'Inspect?' I was startled.

Michael shrugged.

'Yes – to see for themselves what they've done.'

We plunged into that avenue again, as one might into an ocean.

'Do you see those women on the sides?'
I hadn't noticed. Now they were brought to my attention they seemed like torches, tall, shifting from foot to foot, each one at an interval from the other.

'They're from Russia,' said Geeta. 'They come here and are straightaway on the streets, charging two hundred euros by the hour.'

Peter Simons's paths and mine crossed less and less. I'd spot him in the distance: purposeful, modest. He appeared quite contented – as you might when you begin to understand your place in the world.

'We grew up in the free world,' I'd said to him, a bit presumptuous. 'But there was an alternative, wasn't there? And the fact that the "free world" had an alternative made it an alternative itself.' We'd turned this over in our heads, like an equation. '*When freedom is the only reality, you're no longer free.*'

But when I saw him on the street, there was a spring in his step. It was as if being here, and coming into contact again with history – when the East was the West's alternative, and the West (Schöneberg; the town square) the East's – had released him from some constraint.

When we stopped to talk, it was about domestic arrangements. We were neighbours, after all.

Sometimes Dahlem was so quiet that I could hear the silence in the way I could see sunlight in the room. I wasn't miserable. But my need for home made itself present to me – I wasn't conscious of it – through Gerta's arrivals on Friday mornings.

'Dieses Handtuch ist schmutzig,' she called to me from the entrance of the bathroom, holding up a large white towel. 'Ich lege es in die Wäsche.'

I echoed her grave, matter-of-fact expression with a nod and knitted eyebrows, since there was no question of disagreement. We only agreed on everything. I've never had conversations in which I've been in so much harmony with the person I'm talking to.

She smiled, coquettish, implying the joke was on me. 'Schön,' she said; disappeared.

This word I understood. The others I didn't, but I could hear each one distinctly.

After she was done with the noisy bits, the vacuum cleaning, and was wiping the kitchen top – the one thing she undertook as a life-saving task, when I could hear her breathing – I said: 'Do you have plans for the weekend?'

She paused for a second; looked up. 'Das Waschpulver ist fast alle.' She added with a radiant look: 'Mach dir keine Sorgen, ich kaufe neues.'

I felt reassured: happy she was happy.

'We have to do the registration!' Jonas said. He was flustered.

'Registration?'

It turned out I had to register with the police within two months of arrival. I was ignorant of the bureaucracy. The registration was Jonas's lookout. So he was worked up, like a hen puffing up its feathers.

He seized me on my polite weekly trip to the office, and, on Tuesday, we took the U-Bahn from Dahlem-Dorf to Hohenzollernplatz. We walked through glass doors into a sturdy uninviting building, entering without impediment and going straight to the top. I felt out of sorts, as you do – even if you're in perfect health – when you're in a nursing home. Jonas was no-nonsense; he took my passport to make enquiries. A burly man glanced at me while Jonas addressed him.

The queues were puny. We could afford to be distracted. 'See there,' he pointed to the glass windows on the left. I looked at a shore-like expanse, except it was green, tree- and bush-infested, calm. Sometimes, birds rose like specks. 'That's the *entire* stretch of the Tiergarten,' he said, eyes contracting behind the granny glasses. 'Right to the edge of the East. You can see no further.' Matter-of-fact, he said: 'You sense what it felt like in 1989. *That'* – he pointed his head slightly right – 'was as far as you saw. The rest you had to guess at.'

At the end of the queue, I looked deep into the forest. This is what home was: this green darkness. We'd all belonged there. We'd never imagined there was an end to the forest, or that we'd reach the boundary. (The queue lost a person; I moved up.)

Jonas rushed off to lecture. I decided to walk. The stamped form was in my jacket's inner pocket.

I was now *in* the world I'd seen from the top floor; the view had been a reminder of the way it had been portioned out six decades ago. I was forty-three years old – for me, those allotments had been time itself. Then the clock had stopped on reunification. Looking from the Bürgeramt Hohenzollerndamm's top storey at the Tiergarten's expanse, I'd remembered what time was.

Next to the Adenauerplatz U-Bahn station was a store for video rentals. I walked in.

I wondered if I needed to present myself to the woman at the counter. She looked through me. I navigated aisles like the invisible man. Because it was broad daylight, the kind of customer you found within was the sort for whom the store was stopover and residence. I kept my distance: the first room was largest, thick with romances and westerns; the second was stacked with thrillers. The third room was long, well lit, narrow; it contained porn. It had the silence you find in zones that are ambiguous.

A man stood there, head bent, as at a family headstone in a cemetery. On my breezy way back, my eyes caught, among the rows of coloured tablets, a DVD of *Kabhi Khushi Kabhi Gham*. I asked if I could become a member. They needed my passport and stamped police registration form.

'Was the walk all right?'

'Sorry?'

'After registration,' Jonas said.

'Oh yes!'

Registering gave me the liberty to register with the DVD library. I revealed to him I'd borrowed a DVD.

'I take it you've been to the Jewish Museum?'

There was an edge of remonstrance to the words.

'Sorry?'

'The Jewish Museum,' he said, with the calm people have reminding a relative to take medicine.

'No . . . I haven't . . .'

'We *must* go.'

At Hallesches Tor, descending the platform, I walked a path on the fringe of a sixties building.

I arrived at a square with swings and coloured doors. I waited a few moments for one to open; I was lost.

My mobile phone started ringing.

'Are you here?' Jonas was terse. 'The museum is closing.'

I began to run till I reached the main road, from where I ran left. I was perspiring by the time I saw the entrance. Jonas was perspiring too, in his scarf, red, possibly with irritation. He'd bought tickets. We had to display them and offload our overcoats. Our man was young, long-haired, and had a paunch. He had before him a constellation of nationalities, who waited with kindly expressions. They began to move when we reached them.

From floor to floor we went, completing a route, going up the stairs to another. We traced long circles whose outlines weren't clear. Neighbouring us, not far away, was the penultimate drove, going back the way we came, towards final stops. They knew more than we did: we could only guess what by glancing at their faces.

Behind little windows were a handkerchief; a colouring book; a dress. The guide was talking but I didn't need to hear.

In one of the windows was kosher candy. Thin, malleable. A survivor, if categories like 'living' and 'not living' don't apply to the notion of survival.

We broke journey at a panel on the rise and fall of the KaDeWe. It seemed that the museum itself was more like KaDeWe and Peek and Cloppenburg than other museums. I mean it showcases banalities. Where else would you see that except in department stores? Most visitors at KaDeWe are anyway window shoppers. They walk inside and around to look at; not to buy but, marvelling, reconstruct their lives. What else were we doing? I mean no disrespect. But we were in a daydream, going where recognition took us.

Later, we collected our jackets (no point delaying the inevitable) and went to the café to recover. We sat, exhausted, like tramps. We had overcoats on our laps, coffee and slices of cheesecake on the tray.

'I'll get this,' I'd said to Jonas at the till. He'd nodded grimly, still sulking because of my near no-show. Usually he'd say, 'Let me invite you,' German translatorese for 'It's on me.'

I then went to Kreuzberg for dinner – not for the Bangladeshi restaurant, though it was half on my mind, but speculating if the Mercedes-Benz was in the same place.

There were Turkish men standing around. I nodded at those who had nothing to do. I'd grown used to the Turks in the city. Most settled in Kreuzberg when it was a poor area. It used to be poor because it was on the margins of the East and would be among the first to be overrun in case of an invasion. This is what I'd noticed from the top floor in Hohenzollernplatz, looking to the far end of Tiergarten: the idea that the horizon was to be left alone, but it might close in unawares.

I entered a restaurant that looked like a cottage. It reminded me – of what, I wasn't sure. Most things you 'recognise' you've never seen before.

On the same principle, two old Turkish men (possibly related) 'recognised' me. They showed me to a table. On the other hand, they may not have been related except by pallor, stature, and moustache. I sat down and studied

– as you might what's on television – a couple two tables away.

The food was in a buffet. I had to get up and point. I hadn't wanted Indian food, but let myself be guided by resemblances. I settled for something akin to chicken curry, except the gravy had vegetables in it.

The faux cottage gave out an inkling of timelessness and fragility. I couldn't think that the Turkish had been anxious about a possible invasion. They appeared equally unaffected by the possibility's disappearance.

'The Turkish don't integrate. They keep to themselves,' said a lecturer at the comparative literature department when I'd asked him why there were so few Turkish students or faculty at the university. While eating the chicken, I thought about the reluctance to let one experience of displacement and relocation be displaced by another.

I felt like having the rice pudding on display. It *looked* like rice pudding. Bowls were arranged behind a glass. I had seen it in the window of another Turkish restaurant, and had wanted it then. I've never *liked* rice pudding. I never even had a sweet tooth as a child. I may have a sweet tooth now. Berlin gives me licence to experiment.

The rice pudding was minimally sweet – whoever had made it had decided it must look like rice pudding; the rest wasn't his business. It tasted as I'd expected it to: a placid stickiness, not pleasant or unpleasant. One or the other would break the spell.

On my way home, I got off at Rüdesheimer Platz.

I've never alighted at these neighbouring stations – Breitenbachplatz, Rüdesheimer Platz, Heidelberger Platz – but study them when the train pulls up. The walls have no advertisements. They're emblazoned with photos.

The pictures are very busy. Two large women; the hatted men crossing the road; the building coming up (or is it coming down?) – they're what's happening. They haven't already happened.

I get off, look around. There aren't many others. It's ten o'clock. I go up the escalator and feel a slight chill on my cheek. Outside, it's dark, calm. I'm at the wrong stop. I'm surprised at the mismatch between what I saw below and the calm absence I find myself in. Is the absence Rüdesheimer Platz? I think, 'Oskar-Helene-Heim,' and add, 'Idiot!' I go down. I notice the train makes for me from the opposite direction. Wrong platform. I go up again and, crossing from one entrance to another, pass an unresisting membrane. I'm forgetful.

An email came to my inbox – from a sender I didn't know.

'Hello! We met after your inaugural talk, which I enjoyed very much! I love India, I spent three months in Tamil Nadu a couple of years ago. Now I'm on a post-doctoral fellowship and my research area, in fact, is labour movements in South India! I would love to go back. Anyway, Christmas is not far away, and such occasions are always a good excuse to get in touch. I thought I would wish you Merry Christmas and Happy New Year in advance! It would be lovely to see you again. I would be happy to show you around when you are free. Birgit.'

Birgit? I studied the email as if it were *her*. I extrapolated her appearance from the message's shape. I neither trusted the words nor my idle excitement. I'm wary of Europeans who 'love' India – an old neurosis. Christmas was a while from now. Still, I'd never before received an advance Christmas greeting, let alone a Christmas greeting as self-introduction. In my idleness, I thought I'd explore the invitation.

'Dear Birgit, thanks for writing! I'm glad you came to the seminar, and it's good of you to think of me as we approach Christmas. I get the sense that Christmas is brighter and colder in Berlin than in other cities in Europe. But thankfully it's less cold than I thought it would be. It's generous of you to offer to introduce me to parts of the city I may not have seen. I'm happy to be in your charge.'

'I'm happy to be in your charge'! After clicking on the irrevocable 'send', I felt queasy.

An email arrived in twenty minutes.

'Should we meet at 20.00 hrs on Friday at Hackescher Markt? You will need to change at Wittenbergplatz and take the U2 to Zoologischer Garten. From there the U9 will bring you straight to Hackescher Markt.'

I didn't ask her why she wanted me to make this journey. I'd told her I was in her charge.

At the platform, a woman came up to me, a scarf tied round her head. I thought for a second she was a refugee.

'You look like a Muslim woman. I mean you *could* be Arab or Pakistani.'

'Ah, that happens to me at times. A Turkish man will stop and ask for directions. In his language.' She shook her head. 'I wear it for the cold.'

We'd been walking. Introductions weren't necessary. I'm mesmerised by headscarves. In the arcade in the station, a woman was selling Russian dolls. When she saw me looking, she smiled and pulled apart the large doll to reveal the smaller one. I know these dolls, but I looked at her because I wondered if she was Russian. This gave the doll new meaning. When I related this to an English friend, he said he'd visited Hackescher Markt before the wall fell. There were no vendors. 'So much life springs up with trade!' he said. 'Capitalism, huh?'

We went down a long lane. Birgit was a bit in front of me. She was quite tall – as tall as I am.

Couples went in the opposite direction; trailed off. No one belonged; there was a tentativeness in their movements, like they were trespassing. Or as if they were being given access without reason.

I was beginning to tire. 'Here it is!'

A building, with an empty area in the front. As we went nearer, we heard swing music. From the doorway, you could see figures: waiters; but also people dancing. 'It used to be a dance hall,' said Birgit. 'It's a restaurant now, but there is still dancing. Tonight's swing night, I think.'

I'd said I was in her charge; she *was* used to navigating. She gesticulated to a waiter, then spoke into his ear. He nodded, as if receiving orders, and took us to a corner table near the stage. It had a candle and a menu card. We sat down like people who've been expecting good fortune. The stage was full of musical instruments; there was no band. The music was so lifelike I looked twice to check if there was a band on the stage.

'The food is a mix,' Birgit said. 'Mainly German, but with a touch of American.' People danced as we considered the menus.

'Men are such poor dancers,' Birgit said, covering a smile with a hand. 'It would be better if women just danced with women.'

With a little straying, they'd press on us. Closest

was a woman with her back to my gaze, and a bearded forty-year-old, moving with a soft ungainliness. Birgit was right: the woman was lost to her thoughts. She just happened to be dancing. The man was smiling, content, as if he could see he was doing something silly. I smiled too. Like yawns, smiles carry.

'Would you like to?' Birgit asked.

'Sorry?'

'Dance!'

'No!' I burrowed into the menu card.

'I can't force you, but I think you'd be a good dancer.'

'Me?'

'Yes, there's a rhythm to the way you walk – and speak.' I took refuge in the names of courses.

'These people . . . they've been coming here for decades. To dance.'

I wasn't sure what she meant by 'these people'. Were the smiling man and the woman whose face I couldn't see, whose back moved stoically, taking the brunt of his dancing, included? Had they been here *then*? Was it possible to separate then and now? There was a separation, yes, but I was distracted by the wavering figures.

'They've been coming here for twenty years?'

'Yes,' she said, as if saying 'yes' was enough. She believed it the moment she said it. She glanced at the crowd. 'For these dance nights.'

'And was it always this music?'

Her eyes sparkled.

'Yes!'

It wasn't a 'retro' event. The sound in the speakers seemed familiar to people, like a dialect. The numbers moved between country and western, hillbilly and the blues without premeditation. Each was seized as a departure to a different mood. I listened for a hit from the sixties. It didn't come. But the crowd smiled at each song. I began to think the music came from a unique repository: like a record collection you stumble on in someone's home at a certain point in your life.

Studying the dancers – not with envy but absorption, even faint astonishment – I couldn't decide where I was. I wasn't confused. It's just that I didn't feel enough of a divide – between present and past, them and myself. The dance floor had a boundary. The tables were arranged accordingly. But to study the dancers was to be undivided from their world. They just moved; some, like the bearded man, a few steps backward, grinning. The enthusiastic ones twirled. They'd forgotten. This happens with regime change: no vestige of one's history remains. One enters the present anew. Of course, there must be constants: like this music. But it's as if the great changes haven't taken place. Or – this came to me not as a question, but an alternative – had the wall not fallen? Why was I here, in that case?

'When you finish,' said Birgit, busy sorting the food, 'I'll take you up to see something.'
  'Up?'
I had a couple of meat patties to deal with, not quite hamburger, blobs of white sauce on them. On one side

were French fries and a perfunctory garnish of salad.

'Yes,' she said. I connected her provocative smile with the email she'd sent me, wishing me Merry Christmas about a month in advance, and not the local historian she was pretending to be.

'You'll see,' she said, foraging. She was ravenous. My patties didn't taste of very much. I reduced them till only a quarter remained.

'Should we share an apple strudel and cream?' I glanced at the traces of white sauce on the plate. I couldn't imagine not rounding off on dessert.

'You're allowed to have a whole one, you know.' She was thin. I wondered if she was hungry.

'I can't!'

We climbed up with the urgency of childhood friends.

'You see?' she said, placing herself in the middle of the room, waving to her left. There were mirrors on both sides, their lustre dimmed by having to absorb the room without interruption. She was an unsteady axis; I couldn't tell if she was going to try out a dance step. 'Women came here to learn ballroom dancing.' She glanced at the brimming chandelier.

The chairs looked back at me. There are spaces in which you sense time, but also inhabit the viewpoint of those who've already been there. You see through the eyes of those who've gone. These perspectives are intense but momentary.

I turned to find her unsteadily in my proximity.

'You see?' she said.

I wondered what might happen – if we would begin to dance. We were almost circling each other; we were eye to eye.

'It's beautiful,' I said. It reminded me – what could it remind me of? This wasn't my history. But I felt an intimacy, an undecidedness, that had to do with her being nearby.

She moved. She was taller than me – she'd gained a couple of inches, or was floating above the floor. But she also had the angularity of one whose feet are firmly planted.

'Should we go?' Suddenly, she didn't want to linger. The others we'd been were receding. We found we were alone with ourselves.

'I'd love to stay a bit more,' I said, mooning.

She looked over my shoulder.

'But it's getting late,' I said.

We scurried down the stairs.

What happened then I'm not sure. It was late; I thought I'd get a taxi back. It was a long way to the Böll Professor's apartment, but taxis are cheap here. The city's bankrupt; people rent more than they buy; they use taxis as much as they drive. Taxis stay parked near U-Bahn stations, whatever the time of night. I paused before I opened the door. Birgit paused. 'It was lovely!' She leaned forward and, taking us both by surprise, hugged me. It was as if we were preparing to wrestle. She disengaged herself. 'Bye!'

I got back in, and slept.

Next morning, the mobile phone began to ring as I was staring at my toast. When I took the call, there was a Bengali radio voice in my ear.

'Ki, kemon achho?'

I was nonplussed.

'Where have you been?' I made a go of sounding distant.

'Been?' He said he'd got the flu. His tone was breezy. 'Then I was summoned to Moscow,' he explained.

Summoned! He's required everywhere.

I was glad to have him back. We agreed to converge the next afternoon at the Europa Center.

I took the U-Bahn wearing a woollen cap. I had plucked it off a department store in Wittenbergplatz. It had been cold one day in particular last week – Jonas told me it was the coldest in sixty-four years. It had crept on me that evening, a not-unpleasant numbness, making my cheek, when I felt it, feel like a surface that felt nothing itself.

—

Faqrul was wearing a Kashmiri topi. It dwarfed him, like a doll ensconced in a Russian doll. Otherwise, he was lightly dressed. The cap might be a recent acquisition. A Cossack accessory. It had a martial look.

'Ki?' he said. I hadn't asked him anything. Now I did.

'Where are we headed?'

He took me back to the Center from the Tauentzienstrasse entrance. He had a *TLS* from the basement newsagent's under his arm. We criss-crossed the interior till we came out on Budapester Strasse. This road was more functional, silently inhospitable to loiterers.

Still not having responded, he shifted the onus.

'Tumi balo.'

Peering into his palm, he struck a match, took a pull. He flung the match-end in contempt.

Without preamble, he began to recite

ami ekta chhotto deshlaier kathhi
eto naganya, hoyto chokheo podina;
    tobu jeno
mukhe amar ushkhush korchhe barood –
buke amar jole uthbar duranto uchhas . . .

I'm a small matchstick
so insignificant I may not catch your eye;
keep in mind, though,
my mouth bristles with gunpowder –
in my heart's an irresistible urge to burn . . .

Having got that out of his system, he looked pleased. Faqrul will occasionally utter lines from modern Bengali poets. He never quotes himself. We turned left and walked till the 'rotten tooth' was in sight.

'Who's that?' I asked.

'Aar ke – Sukanta,' as to an imbecile he'd been given charge of.

It came to me:

'It's odd, just how many of the political poems are about things you find in the home – even in the kitchen. Matchsticks, burnt bread, boiled rice.'

'Rotten tooth!' he said grandly.

He says it each time we walk past the structure. Its crown is damaged, but the tooth's no more in pain. Its nerve-endings are dead. Berlin, over here, is a mouth left open.

But we didn't go anywhere. We circled Kurfürstendamm. I bought paracetamol and toothpaste. Faqrul was like a chaperone during these purchases, making sure I wasn't overcharged – as if we were in a market in Dhaka.

Over tea, I spoke of Birgit.

'Bir-git,' he murmured. Names were a key to the person and their world.

Then he came to himself.

'Why don't you bring her along to dinner on Friday?' Expansive and insistent. He believed in nothing as much as making an impression. 'There is a very good place on Eisenacher Strasse.' It wasn't easy for him to say 'Eisenacher Strasse'. I recalled the respect he commanded in Bangladeshi restaurants.

I didn't know her well enough to pass on the invitation. Besides, I wasn't sure she'd want to widen her social circle.

'Would you like to come home for dinner?' This query was put to me independent of Faqrul's machinations. It showed up in my inbox a day after my Wittenbergplatz sojourn. 'Where do you live? I'd love to, of course,' I wrote after a hiatus. 'I'm in Ostkreuz,' she replied that afternoon. 'You can take the train straight to Warschauer Strasse. It shouldn't be more than 35 minutes. Thursday?'

The train is sturdy, crowded. It's a wonder it doesn't fall apart. It rattles. The outside becomes darker station to station, maybe because light goes fast this time of the year. The sky is pale, though. Warschauer Strasse is larger than I thought; my heart sinks as the train slows. But, because it's a terminus, I'm caught up in its churning, its mass segues. I find myself on a bridge, looking below to where I came from, then ahead to where the bridge continues.

'You keep going down that bridge,' says Birgit (I disguise the apprehensiveness in my voice), ''till you come to a tunnel. At the end of the tunnel you turn left.'

It's extraordinary how close her home is. As soon as I go into the tunnel, the sky disappears. I become confident. I no longer feel lacking in directions – I know my way. In the meantime, lights have come on. I'm soothed by the young people coming towards me, heading out. They're angelic. Are there any old people in Ostkreuz? When I emerge, the pale sky doesn't trouble me. It's cordoned off by buildings.

Birgit has something in the pot. She lives on the third floor. I climb up, savouring narrowness.

'It's Italian,' she says, poking her head into the kitchen as if checking on an infant. 'Vegetarian. I hope you don't mind.'

'Not at all,' I lie.

'I'm not vegan any more. I crossed a threshold one day – enough tofu, I thought.' She laughs, reminiscing, self-absorbed. Her hair glows. There's a small piano to the right, bought cheap from a sale. It's here, but it's still a bit of another home. At the room's end is a window. A desk is placed before it. On the left of the window, incumbents, a CD player and speakers. Along the wall, coming out from the shadow, a small sofa. I sit. I find myself sliding.

'Are you tired?' she asks, politely concerned. 'Are you hungry?'

'Not at all!' I protest. 'Your hair's changed,' I say in mock puzzlement.

A mysterious smile appears. It brings to mind the person who wished me a premature Merry Christmas.

'Henna.' She's amused. Her primary source of amusement is herself. 'I like henna.'
I'm duly agog.

'I got henna last week from Wedding,' she explains. A chain of speculations is set off by her pronunciation. 'Vey-ding.' I connect this in a few seconds to a name on road signs. At first I read it without thinking, as you do words that are familiar. Then I admitted it must be a place – a location for celebrations.

'What is Wedding?' I ask, wishing to resolve the matter.

'It has interesting shops,' she says, returning from the kitchen. 'You must go there. I buy henna there. Indian spices.'

Hermit-like, she vanishes. She's already put on eighties glam rock. She insists I listen – 'It's a shame you never paid attention to this: it's very plangent.' Of all decades,

I'm happiest to dispense with the eighties. Birgit recoils; that was when she came out of dormancy. She's intent on educating me: 'But the eighties were extraordinary!' She's hurt; I give in. I get up, explore the room. I tap out notes on the piano. I can't play, but its keys ring true. I go to the desk, press down on it. There are apartments opposite. Rather than being an observer, I tend to enter the lives of things I see. I'm now in *that* building. Mimicking myself, I look back from there to this window. I become a detail. When I move my gaze, I notice a man and a woman in a flat diagonally across. They're cooking. The man bends to kiss her on the neck. Their universe is self-sufficient. They can't conceive of being watched; they think everyone is as deep in their world as they are. The woman tilts her head. Might they make love? I look away.

I'm at the entrance of Birgit's bedroom. It's next to the window, lit with a faint pink light. Against a wall is a mirror with a bone-white frame. I imagine her looking into it. When you notice mirrors in other people's homes, you don't stare into them without seeing them. You encounter them as objects, as part of a fabric.

Birgit is standing beside me.

'I love that mirror,' she says. I follow her in.

I shiver.

'It's cold in here.'

'I like my bedroom cold. I can't sleep when it's warm.'

'Do you play?'

I indicate the piano. Her glance is disavowing.

'I sing.'

It's as if she's admitting to royal blood. She smiles evasively to counter her words.

'You do?'

'Oh, not well! But I make songs.'

'Sing one! What kind of songs?' The heavy metal anthem is sobbing on low volume.

She gets up and takes possession of the stool. I rise.

> Die Welt ist voller Liebe
> sie ist voller Liebe
> Keine Zeit zu trauern
> Nein, keine Zeit

Her voice is tremulous – unremarkable; pleasant. Her expression is open-mouthed, startled, as if a ghost had put a hand on her shoulder. She stops after a stanza. It's not as if a spell is broken. Abruptly, she's now someone else: cheerfully inadequate to the demands of laying a table.

———

'Mmmm.'

I feel fraudulent chewing on vegetables. I'm not convinced they're real food. A heap coloured by Parmesan and pesto, mixed with fettuccine.

'Next time, I'll make daal,' she says, as if she's consulted a crystal ball.

I see myself in the bedroom's pink glow. I see her pale body in the mirror. I have no inkling of what might happen next.

I realise, later, I've seen many Birgits. They splayed across the evening like playing cards, some of which I studied more closely than others. Or it was as if smaller dolls had emerged from a Russian doll over two hours, each the same as the original, but, seen at different spots in the room, requiring fresh perspectives.

After dinner, we listened to a bit more music. It sounded autochthonic now, the 80s rock: something that emanated from a cave. There was a process of conversion going on, a waiting and seeing if I was ready to enter the cave with her.

On my way back, I'm lost briefly before I find the tunnel. This has been happening – not the loss of a sense of direction, but a dispensing with memory of recent events and things I've grown up with. For instance, it occurs to me that, while I discussed food with Birgit, and music, I told her very little of my life. It wasn't as if I kept my life from her. I simply forgot about it. It was like it never happened. When I'm lost these days, as I am on my way to Warschauer Strasse, I don't feel anxious because the streets are familiar. Where I find myself is related to the return of some old memory. I don't know what the memory is, but I recognise where I am. On the other hand, I'd say the world I belonged to, the one I came from, has little veracity any more. It began to vanish in the eighties and nineties. I don't feel lost in Berlin – here, I'm in the present. I'd say the same of Faqrul: that, if he went back home, he wouldn't find it there. There's more of that home in Berlin now – in Wittenbergplatz; Görlitzer Bahnhof. We have an appetite for home, as flies do for food. We find it unerringly.

It's snowing. When I return from university, I see the grass around the building is two inches white. I step in, wondering if my boots will withstand the plunge. I leave behind crevasses.

The Böll Professor's apartment is an oasis. Grunewald approaches. Like my shoes, the apartment is impermeable.

Birgit calls.

'Have you seen *Kabhi Khushi Kabhi Gham*?'

I think I've heard of it, I say.

'You *think* you've heard of it! Where have you been all these years?'

She tells me it's a favourite film as if that were a category whose meaning is universal. Does she have a taste in irony? Auburn hair; *this*?

'I have a DVD player,' I say, quailing at the thought of being imprisoned for three hours with *Kabhi Khushi Kabhi Gham*.

'Let me see if I can find my copy,' she intervenes.

99

I tell her I've joined a DVD library at Adenauerplatz.

'I think I can get hold of it.'

She'll be in Dahlem tomorrow. I say exactly where the Böll Professor's flat is, put my key under the mat. When I come back with the video, it's dark. I step into snow again.

She's on the sofa, clearly at home. She's taken her shoes off – right leg crossed, foot on sofa. The rest of her is unaware of the foot and turned marginally to me.

'Did you get the video?'
She's increasingly direct. Already addressing me as hunter-gatherer.

'Do you want to watch the film or eat first?'

'We can eat and watch.'
I have Indian takeaway for the evening: aubergine, daal, rice; chicken for me. We swirl food on our plates in the film's first fifteen minutes. Aubergine stains rice while daal leaks in several directions. Soon – I've yet to see Birgit not hungry – there's nothing on the plate but stains.

'What is it about this movie that appeals?'
It's as if I'm on a long flight, and am curious about what I'm doing.

'I think what we' – 'we' I infer as 'Germans' – 'love

about Bollywood is the importance of family. It speaks to us. We've lost our sense of family. We're alone.' She moves one leg down, the other up. She smiles whenever Kareena Kapoor struts into the frame as she does when relating oddities in her day.

I don't dismiss the words. Cliché is often the strongest way to convey a truth.

'Where are you from? Did you grow up in Berlin?'

'No,' she says. 'In a village near Hannover. You wouldn't have heard of it. It's by a river.' She smiles. 'I'm glad to be away.'

I envision her childhood. Whenever I focus, it's the same music and set of expressions. The film allows me back in. It's open house.

She goes to the bathroom. For a long time. The Böll Professor's bathroom is a different country – she may find she's in thrall and want to linger.

Back in the drawing room, she says:

'It's late.'

Barefoot, shorn.

'Can I stay the night?'

I study her face. My mind goes blank – not in the way it went blank when I was staring at the TV.

'I'm not feeling as well as I should,' she continues, grim. 'I've been having . . . I had . . . you know . . . I thought it would end today but it hasn't.' She makes a face.

'There's an extra bed and room!' Rarely entered except by Gerta. 'It's cold and late! You shouldn't go!'

She smiles, reminiscent.

'I don't have anything to wear, though . . .' she murmurs, casting glances around her. 'I'm sorry . . .'

'Kurta? Will a kurta do?'

She mulls over the word.

'I *love* kurtas.'

We relax.

After ten minutes, she's back in the diaphanous top. It stops above her knees. She herself seems to hover above the ground.

'Does it fit?'

It's a rhetorical question. She ignores it; floats to the kitchen.

After two days, we meet, like diplomats drawing out an issue, near the Zoologischer Garten. Birgit's shifted orbit. We walk to – where else – Wittenbergplatz. The shoe shops; the first floor of the Hugendubel, where you can sit for hours with a book; the rotten tooth – everything is a monument here. Nothing is. We stand, undecided.

I spot wagonloads of bratwurst. Pre-Christmas festivity, light, and flame. The würstchen has moved from near the Wittenbergplatz U-Bahn towards the rotten tooth. Faqrul passed on the news. 'You must go there. Now is the time!' he said, his voice lit with craving for haraam. That's why I'm here. I think: 'Birgit's vegetarian.'

We explore by-lanes; find a handsome, unvisited Chinese restaurant. We order in solitude: soup and fried noodles. Birgit will never not be thin. She eats significantly more than me, but I wonder if she eats when she's alone.

We emerge as if the paparazzi had wind of us. We stride forward. There's no one on the street. It's cold.

Half-empty Ku'damm sparkles.

Uhlandstrasse is shabby. It lacks the sharpness that freezing temperatures bring.

Women stand near the U-Bahn entrance. They have the furtiveness of people who pretend they're busy in order not to work.

'You know who they are, don't you,' says Birgit, lowering her head like she's at a social gathering.

I glance with vagueness.

'They turn up at this time.'

She's smiling. She's remembering, or has an intimation.

'I was here, deciding which U-Bahn to take. An Arab came to— maybe thought I was from his part of the world.' She lifts eyebrows to the headscarf. 'He asked me how much I'd charge.'

'You mean—' My responses are phlegmatic. I ascertain which feels more foreign, the story or our soft conversation.

'These Arabs . . .' She smiles at the impetuosity.

Why would an Arab presume a woman in a hijab is on the job?

'Let's pretend for five minutes,' I say. We've been on the stairs, uncertain, as if something were holding us back from descending.

'Pretend?'

'You know . . . I'll come back in two minutes.'

'All right.' She says this on a second's consideration. The game's begun.

I shuffle round the awning. Two women gaze at me, expectant and without interest. For someone doing business, a person doesn't qualify as a customer till they display signs. I get back in less than a minute. She's angular; defending herself from a breeze. She's changed her spot.

'Are you . . .'

She assesses me, non-committal.

'How much?'

Silent. Then:

'One hundred.' Imperious. Non-negotiable.

I protest.

'I don't have that much money!'

At Wittenbergplatz U-Bahn, there's excitement on plat-
forms. Groups descend; couples get off. People shout
across the tracks.

Uhlandstrasse is desolate. We're the only two in the
compartment. Birgit drapes the scarf round her shoulders.

At Wittenbergplatz, we merge into the melee for
Line 3.

'Where will you sleep, then?' I ask.
I hang on to our make-believe but acknowledge the fact
that she was here two nights ago.

'You call the shots,' she says. Is she still playing?

'Go in there,' I say, pointing to the little room. 'You'll
find a kurta.'

'You want me to wear it?'

I, at least, sleep deeply. When I get up to go to the toilet,
I see a ghost-like figure near me, breathing. The kurta is
torn at the pocket.

I hear the train's long-drawn-out horn whenever it
passes.

I wake up alone. 9 a.m. The blanket's tousled.

From the passage, I lean forward, survey the drawing room. Then, cursorily, I enter the toilet. It's filled with daylight.

When I emerge, I expect her to be on the sofa. There's no one there. I proceed to the kitchen, disoriented by the prospect of having coffee and toast. Am I getting it wrong? Did I miss something?

I butter the dark bread, which tastes the same toasted or untoasted. I ponder upon the coffee mug.

Whom did I bring home last night? I try her number.

Finding the rooms empty, I even gaze into the closet, below the hangers, in case she crept in for some time to herself. It's not implausible. People claim spaces without explanation.

A woman comes out of the small room. What's her name? I know her. She's sixty or older, tall – hefty, actually. She has a white dress on. She comes out, displaying a small bundle. My kurta.

'Soll ich das in die Wäsche legen?'
She's lowered her head, like a bull. Her eyes are trained on me.

I say Yes to her in English. I always say Yes. She nods, resolute. Her hair is white. Into the bathroom she goes.

The name will come back, but it doesn't matter when. I know I trust her.

Easterners don't know English – but they understand Yes.

I go to Uhlandstrasse. Afternoon. I do a recce. It's not that I expect Birgit to be there: I'm looking for some kind of confirmation.

The women, as is to be expected, have gone. Calm dreariness reigns. People walk into pharmacies; they confabulate in cafés.

Warschauer Strasse's an extremity. I go there to get my bearings. By now, she's an excuse. I'm looking for her, but I'm also curious about where the world goes in the evening. She can't be in this crowd.

The trains emanate sorrow. Not like humans. The humans, in fact, are distracted and impatient. The trains aren't alive in the way we understand the word. But they feel.

Domination of steel: steel smoke, steel sky.

I walk around, no longer looking for Ostkreuz. I'm lost again, but not exercised. I can turn round any time. The trains go to Oskar-Helene-Heim.

I must have blacked out. I'm not sure if it was the Warschauer Strasse evening or another one. There's a memory of the moment. Gigantic figures above. Men in hats, crossing a road; a woman in a skirt that came down to her feet.

When I opened my eyes, I didn't know where I was. People were helping me up from the platform. The past had let go of me. The present was a flicker. Those hatted men were unmindful of being very close.

I've blacked out again. I'm awake now. This is a ward. The walls and scent of disinfectant are placating.

Someone's speaking Bangla. 'Ja bitte!' 'Ich bin froh, dass es ihm gut geht!' It's German, of course. I'm immersed in the gaucheness of the accent. The voice hisses suddenly – a smoker's laugh.

The second time, I have stitches on my forehead. I recall the men in moustaches and hats crossing the road in Rüdesheimer Platz. I mention them to no one.

I'm no longer definite about how I met Birgit – or if she came with me that night from Uhlandstrasse. Was it another? I don't have the energy to check the veracity of the details in my inbox.

Jonas calls.

'Are you okay?'

'Sorry?'

'The word in the department is you aren't well. Can I take you to see a doctor?'

I dig my heels into the Böll Professor's apartment.

'It's ok, Jonas. It's been fixed.'

'I'm sorry – what's been fixed?'

'The dizzy spells.'

Jonas retreats. He's deciding whether to trust me.

'Are you sure?'

'Very.'

Gently he points out I missed last week's class.

'But don't let that worry you! The students will be relieved to hear you're well!'

I reread *A Personal Matter*. I place my backside each day on the spot where Oe descended; why not relive his life? The writing's untidy; unbridled. Oe must be difficult. I'm surprised how placid-looking he is.

I haven't kept track of the weeks, but I need to take *Kabhi Khushi Kabhi Gham* back. I can't bear to look at the DVD's cover, the photoshopped red of the saris.

I must have run up an insurmountable fine.

It's bright, and, at the library's counter, the light comes in impure – not with winter's clarity. They hardly see me. I get a generic nod. There's no fine.

As I go down the U-Bahnhof, I hear music. It's too far away to identify its ethnicity. I recognise it for being beautiful and alien, and, as I walk into the passage, am trying to understand what it is that speaks to me. A woman is singing. The song's ascending in mid-air; the instrumentation's weightless: strings, a horn. It's louder now. An Indian fruit vendor's playing it on a radio. I don't know this song.

This morning, I don't know my name. Half an hour goes by. It's on the tip of my tongue. I overhear the buzz of other names – Oe; Böll Professor. Not mine. It'll come to me. I'm puzzled by the lapse but more puzzled by why I need this information.

'Birgit bhalo?'

He remembers her! He's never seen her. But, dropping the name with sly presumptuousness, he anoints her presence.

'I don't know – haven't heard.'

He clears his throat.

'I'll take you both to a restaurant on Eisenacher Strasse – the owner's a chela of mine.'

It's as if she and I are married.

I reconsider the name – my name. I'm in the pharmacy buying vitamins. The name hadn't gone away. No one *remembers* their name: it's there, like your face. I do a check on it in the pharmacy as with a language you knew as a child but stopped using. Because hardly anyone addresses me by name these days but Jonas. Faqrul's indirect, like a bridegroom is with his bride.

It's less cold today. I want to step onto a balcony.

Birgit calls.

'Hello?'

I know the voice.

'I'm sorry.'

I don't want explanations. She says she got a text at dawn – her mother was ill. She left without waking me. She went to the village near Hannover. She left her phone behind on the train.

'So stupid!'

Jonas enquires if there are any sights I'd like to see, given I won't be here in a month's time. Just as there was an inaugural talk, there will be a farewell event. I'll also have dinner with the head of the department, Professor Morgenthau.

I'm in Oranienburger Strasse. I notice the restaurants with tables on the pavement are shielded by plastic sheeting and burn within. I call Birgit.

'What about Indian food?'

'Indian food? Where are you?'

'Oranienburger Strasse. Besides, I'd like to say bye.'

'Can you give me half an hour?'

She's moved to staid Charlottenburg.

We hug briefly, to subdue suspicion. We're still not sure we like each other. We choose a table outside.

The restaurant's cocooned by sheeting. We sit by an oven. The heat on my cheek's intolerable.

'So – is she better?'

She looks uncomprehending, more concerned with finding her balance on the chair.

'Your mother.'

Her face lights up with a kind of relief.

'Yes! She could have died!'

We study the menus, as if we've been told to.

A man steps up.

'Can you give us two minutes?'

The restaurant's smartly Orientalist; not like the derelict palaces Faqrul took me to. Very likely there'll be more of these on Oranienburger Strasse; more flute and sitar.

I yawn.

'Thank you!' she says. 'I didn't realise I was so interesting.'

'No, no – it's the fire, I think.' I check the embers.

We're in a battle tent. 'I haven't been sleeping well. It comes over me at some points in the day.'

'I can't imagine you're a sound sleeper,' she says, turning the hardboard page. 'There's something fitful about you.'

I've thrown off my jacket; she her scarf. My chest is sticky.

'You remind me of someone.' It takes a lot to say this; it's come to me now.

She waits for me to complete the thought.

There's korma and pilau in front of us. The cream subsumes other colours.

'When you wear that scarf, I mean. I knew a girl in college who covered her head. I thought of her when I first saw you in Hackescher Markt.'

'You'd know many women who wear headscarves, no?'

'Not really.'

We turn the food over.

I tell her how we grew close – this woman and I. We deepened our friendship knowing it had no future – because of our religious denominations, and the fact that she wouldn't transgress against her parents.

'I like the story.' Her eyes are pale.

We sit after the plates have been removed. It's not laziness; we're clinging to inertia. As if the battle starts tomorrow, and we're engrossed till it does.

I want to make love but won't say it outright. We wait without purpose on the street. I turn away to belch. The spices are from a journey made in a dream, hinting at another reality.

'Well?'

'Well?'

I defer to the thought of the mother – convalescing in a village near Hannover.

'I hope she's better soon.'

She looks at me, disbelieving.

'Is that it?'

'I hope not,' I say. 'I hope it isn't.'

'The last two weeks have left me tired.'

I wander off, a vagrant.

I gravitate towards the dome. I feel a pull; not to one thing – in different directions.

I know this part of the city from my childhood. The sturdy corner buildings; the crossroads – I've gone from one side of the road to the other many times. I know the crossing. Or maybe I don't know it. It's new, and old.

I keep walking – in which direction I'm not sure; Kreuzberg? I've lost my bearings – not in the city; in its history. The less sure I become of it, the more I know my way.

I stand before a building. It's functional. It can't possibly have a view. Its balconies are blue.

I don't have a key. No one stirs – not even a dog. I consider sitting on the pavement.

'Du bist wach!'

The woman's studying me. I've opened my eyes and the sun rushes in. She's glancing at me while hanging up clothes.

I'm in a chair. The balcony across the street is blue.

'Ich habe dich unten gefunden. Du warst eingeschlafen.' She's as I remember: large and white-haired. She hooks the chemise to the clothesline.

I nod. I feel sad – she's led this life for years.

I have my routines. I'll manage them in a moment. The paucity of choices, the familiar parameters – I don't question them. I'll probably die before anything changes.

Acknowledgements

I'm grateful to Alex Bowler, Emmie Francis, Edwin Frank, and Meru Gokhale for their support, and to Alex and Emmie for their editorial attention.

I should thank Silvia Crompton for her meticulous copy-edits.

I'm very grateful to Indira Ghose and Souvik Mukherjee for help with the German.

Sarah Chalfant, Jessica Bullock, Alba Ziegler-Bailey – my thanks for your role in seeing the book through.

Rinka, who continues to be the first reader of the MS; Radha, for being there.